THE
CLASS PICTURE DAY
FROM THE
BLACK LAGOON®

HA, HA, HA!

Get more monster-sized laughs from

The Black Lagoon®

THE
CLASS PICTURE DAY
FROM THE
BLACK LAGOON®

CLICK!

by Mike Thaler
Illustrated by Jared Lee

SCHOLASTIC INC.

For Judi and Susan:
above and beyond
—M.T.

To Johnnie and Carol Wolfe
—J.L.

GIANT
COOTIE →

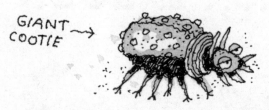

ISBN 978-0-545-47666-9

Text copyright © 2012 by Mike Thaler
Illustrations copyright © 2012 by Jared D. Lee Studio, Inc.

12 11 10 9 8 7   16 17/0

Printed in the U.S.A.   40
First printing, October 2012

TWO COOTIES
AND A GNAT → · · ·

RUBBER SNAKE

FAKE ↗
TONGUE

CONTENTS

TWO COOTIES,
ONE GNAT, AND ⟶ . . . .
A TINY BALL

PIRANHAS

CHAPTER 1
AS PRETTY AS A PICTURE

Mrs. Green says that this Friday is class *picture day*. I don't look good in photos—I'm better in person. But she says we all have to have our picture taken. Well, if we have to . . . I want to look my very best. Actually, even better than my best.

I want to look great! A handsome heroic Hubie hunk.

I need a miracle by Friday. That's only three days away. I better start combing my hair now.

PLASTIC BIRD →

PLASTIC COMB →

CAN I CHEW ON YOUR COMB WHEN YOU'RE DONE?

REAL BUG ↓

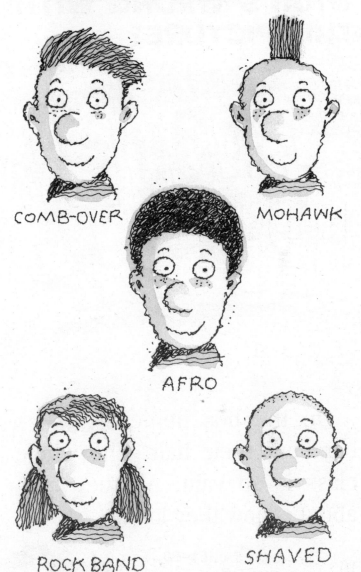

CHAPTER 2
WHAT'S WRONG WITH THIS PICTURE?

On the bus home *everyone's* combing their hair. The whole class is so vain. All they care about is how they look.

10   HUBIE'S CHEWED-
UP COMB   →

It's only a picture, and beauty is only skin-deep. Boy, I hope I've got thick skin.

A RHINO HAS VERY THICK SKIN ↗

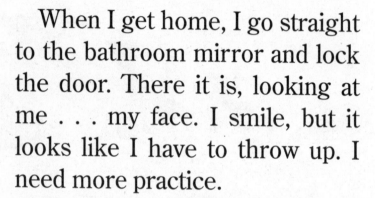

CHAPTER 3
MIRROR, MIRROR

When I get home, I go straight to the bathroom mirror and lock the door. There it is, looking at me . . . my face. I smile, but it looks like I have to throw up. I need more practice.

There are different kinds of smiles:

There's the show-all-your-teeth
hyena smile.
No!

There's the nuts-in-your-cheeks
chipmunk smile.
No!

SMILING
BUG $\longrightarrow$

There's the "I don't care" nonchalant casual cool *lips-tight smile*.
No!

There's the "I know something you don't know" *sly-snake smile*.
No!

There's the "I'm sorry" *elephant smile*, and the "I haven't got a clue" *hippo smile*.

Mom knocks on the door. "Hubie, what are you doing in there?"

"Smiling, Mom."

It's quiet for a minute.

"Smiling at what?" she finally asks.

I open the door. "For the school picture." I smile again.

That's it!

The *smiling-at-Mom smile*.

16

CHAPTER 4
THE TIME MACHINE

BEING THEMSELVES →

"What's the big deal, Hubie? Just be yourself, be natural," says Mom.

"I don't know what natural is for me," I say.

CONFUSED →

HOW TO LOOK NATURAL

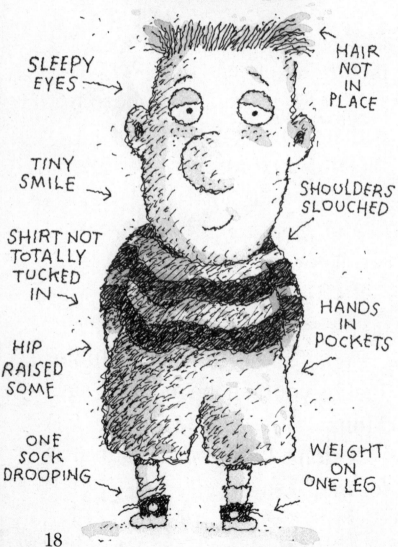

SLEEPY EYES →

HAIR NOT IN PLACE

TINY SMILE →

SHOULDERS SLOUCHED

SHIRT NOT TOTALLY TUCKED IN →

HANDS IN POCKETS

HIP RAISED SOME

ONE SOCK DROOPING →

WEIGHT ON ONE LEG

"You're a very handsome young man . . . just be yourself."

"That's easy for you to say, Mom. You never had to have your picture taken at school."

Mom gets up and comes back with a photo album.

"Oh, but I did," she says, opening to the first page.

And there, smiling at me, was my mom in the third grade.

It's amazing—my mom was once a kid!

CHAPTER 5
BEAUTY AND THE BEAST

That was interesting, but I'm still stuck with the same problem. I find an article in one of Mom's magazines called "10 Days to a More Beautiful You." I only have two days—I better get started.

20 ← EYE   EYELASHES ↓

DIRT + WATER = MUD

Step 1. *The mud pack.*

No problem.

I go to the backyard. There's a lot of mud. I put it on my face. Hey, this is going to be easy!

HARD-HAT AREA.

WATER HOSE

Step 2. *The cucumber facial.*

I go to the fridge. I can't find a cucumber, but I find a jar with one pickle left. Close enough. I cut it into thin slices and put them all over my face. They stick to the mud. Tailspin sees me and runs out of the room.

Step 3. *The hairnet.*

I find Mom and ask her if I can borrow her hairnet. She screams!

"Is that you, Hubie? What are you doing?"

I show her the magazine article.

"Mom, I'm only on step two."

"Well, *step to* the bathroom and wash your face," she says.

PICKLE

← MUD

23

"But, Mom, I only have two days to become a more beautiful me."

"Young man, you only have two minutes to wash your face and come to dinner."

MUD →

← PICKLE

24

CHAPTER 6
A THOUSAND WORDS

At dinner, I practice my smile. "Please pass the cheese, please."

"You're acting very strange, Hubie," Mom says, passing the cheese.

"Do not freeze the fleas in the cheese."

WHAT ARE YOU TALKING ABOUT?

CHEESE ↓

FLEAS →

BONE →

"Hubie, do you have a fever?" Mom asks.

"I'm practicing my smile. I'm doing smile exercises. The trees have knees that wheeze in the breeze."

"Hubie!"

"Hey, Mom, would you like some pickles?"

"Are those the ones that were on your face?"

"It's okay . . . I washed 'em." I smile.

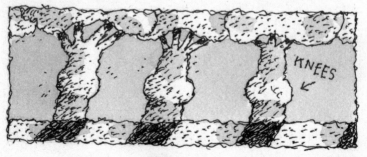

KNEES

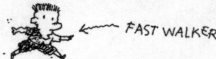

FAST WALKER

26

SMILE EXERCISES

UP

DOWN

OPEN

CLOSE

STRETCH

RESULTS

27

TRUCK DRIVEN BY A GNAT →

CHAPTER 7
FEATURE
PRESENTATION

I NEED TO GO OUTSIDE.

After dinner, I look in another magazine.

One article says to "find your best feature and feature it!"

I look in the mirror. My nose—definitely, my nose is my best feature.

WHAT TIME ARE YOU GOING TO THE POND?

DON'T BE SO NOSY!

29

30

CAR DRIVEN BY A GNAT

CHAPTER 8
WHO NOSE?

POP!

BARK!
BARK!

That night I have a dream. I'm a clown in the circus. I have a big red nose. But suddenly it flies away and lands on the fat lady. I try to catch it, but it flies to the thin man. I run after it, but it moves on to the strong man.

Next, it goes to the lion tamer, and then on to the lion. I try to catch it with a butterfly net, but it lands on the elephant. I sit down and cry, but it's hard to cry without a nose. It flies down and lands on me and the circus goes on. I wake up and look in the mirror.

My nose is still there, all right.
But there's a big red pimple right
on the end of it!

NOSEDIVE →

CHAPTER 9
TAKING SIDES

On the school bus, everyone is smiling—practicing, I guess. Who am I kidding? They're all looking at the end of my nose. They're all staring at it.

"My right side's my best side." Eric smiles. "What's yours?"

Oh, no, I never picked my best side.

"The back of my head?" I ask.

"No," says Eric.

LOST BUG

"What do you think?" I ask, turning my head from side to side.

"Neither!" he says.

34

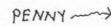

PENNY ⟶

I stop smiling.

"Just kidding," says Eric. "They're both totally awesome. What do you think, Doris?"

She looks at me hard.

"The inside," she says.

Now *there's* a girl with heart.

We take a vote and it's a tie. I guess that's good—it's the middle that's the problem.

DORIS →

YOU CHOOSE

RIGHT SIDE

LEFT SIDE

FRONT SIDE

BACK SIDE

CHAPTER 10
DO'S AND DONUTS

In class, Mrs. Green gives us a list of picture-day do's and don'ts.

Don't:

GUM

1. Pick your nose
2. Cross your eyes
3. Chew gum
4. Blink
5. Wink
6. Smirk
7. Jerk
8. Stick out your tongue
9. Frown
10. And absolutely no rabbit ears

DON'T PICK YOUR NOSE.

DO I HAVE A NOSE?

Eric raises his hand.

"Yes, Eric?" Mrs. Green says.

"What if you're a rabbit?" He giggles.

Mrs. Green clears her throat and continues.

Do:
1. Put your hands at your sides
2. Face the camera
3. Say "Cheese"

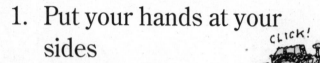

At lunch, everyone has a cheeseburger.

We all said "Cheese!" We were practicing.

CHEESE

OTHER DON'TS

DON'T WIGGLE YOUR EARS

DON'T LOOK DOWN AT THE FLOOR

DON'T SMILE IF YOU ARE MISSING A FRONT TOOTH

DON'T CROSS YOUR FINGERS

DON'T SCRATCH, EVEN IF YOU HAVE POISON IVY

DON'T TAP YOUR TOES

DON'T SWIVEL YOUR HIPS.

DON'T SNIFF, EVEN IF YOU HAVE A COLD ⟶

41

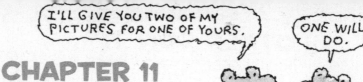

CHAPTER 11
SIX PICS

That afternoon, the class is wheeling and dealing! Everyone is making deals like "I'll give you my picture if you give me yours."

I've got orders for six pictures.
Randy's not smiling.

"What's the matter?" I ask.

"Nobody wants my picture,"
he says.

WHY THE FROWN?

"I want your picture." I say,
smiling. "In fact, I'll take six of
them."

Sometimes it's so easy to make
someone happy.

SORRY THIS IS TAKING
SO LONG.

CHAPTER 12
CLOTHES MAKE THE MAN

Tomorrow's the big day. I spend the whole afternoon picking out my *war*drobe. I wonder why they don't call it a *peace*drobe. Maybe it's because you have to fight for what you want to wear.

Freddy says not to wear stripes 'cause they make you look bigger. Derek says not to wear yellow 'cause it makes you look pale.

Eric says he's going to put a hat in front of his face like the gangsters do. He's kidding . . . I think.

BIG FREDDY

PALE DEREK

PRETTY-BOY ERIC

Mom says to wear a tie. I'd rather die than wear a tie. So much for peace! We call a truce—I'll wear a belt.

My wardrobe is all laid out. I even cleaned my sneakers in the dishwasher.

MOM'S SUGGESTIONS

GREASED-DOWN ← HAIR

MAKEUP TO HIDE PIMPLE →

STARCHED LONG-SLEEVE WHITE SHIRT WITH BUTTON-DOWN COLLAR ←

DESIGNER TIE →

PRESSED KHAKI SHORTS →

← BELT

BRIGHT WHITE SNEAKERS →

DARK SOCKS

CHAPTER 13
BEAUTY REST

I go to bed early to get my beauty rest. I don't want bags under my eyes.

I keep going over my possible poses: bold, heroic, Mr. America, sympathetic, intense, dramatic, serious, confident, relaxed, laid-back, nonchalant . . . Finally, I fall asleep.

BAGS→

I'm a famous movie star. Everyone wants my picture. The cameras don't stop flashing. People take pictures of me all day. I smile so much my teeth hurt.

When I go swimming, they use underwater cameras. When I jump up in the air, they use aerial photography. They even take pictures while I'm asleep.

There goes a flash now! I open my eyes, but it's only the sun coming in the window. It's picture day!

CLICK! CLICK!

I'VE SEEN ALL OF YOUR MOVIES.

CHAPTER 14
A HAIR-RAISING EXPERIENCE

I get out of bed and go to the mirror. Uh-oh, it's a bad hair day. Nothing I do holds it down. I should have worn a hairnet.

Oh, no! There's still a pimple on the end of my nose.

This is going to be a disaster. I'll be immortalized as a mess. What will future generations think?

PIMPLE→ • WART→ •

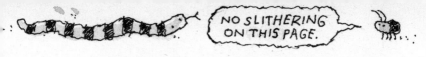

NO SLITHERING ON THIS PAGE.

"I bet that kid broke the camera," they'll say, laughing.

Well, at least my teeth will be white. I brush them six times.

I put on clean underpants. I'm not sure why or how they will affect the picture—it was Mom's idea.

I eat breakfast carefully, but I still get a spot on my shirt.

Spots are my destiny. They seek me out like missiles. Oh, well. Off to picture day.

HUBIE'S POSES

BOLD

HEROIC

RELAXED

INTENSE

SERIOUS

CHAPTER 15

PICTURE PERFECT

When the school bus pulls up, I don't recognize anybody. They're all clean and combed and wearing their best clothes.

FREDDY

PENNY

DORIS

RANDY

Freddy has on a tie, Penny and Doris both have perms, and Randy got a haircut.

YOU'VE GROWN ANOTHER LEG.

NO, I'M WEARING A TIE.

Everyone sits very still. They don't want one hair to move. I stick my head out the window ... mine couldn't get any worse than it already is.

CHAPTER 16
A SNAPPY SHOT

At school, we all line up and march down to the gym. I make sure I'm at the end of the line. A big camera is all set up and there are lots of bright lights. It looks like an operating room.

I feel like I'm going in for surgery.

Mrs. Green reviews the picture-taking do's and don'ts.

Penny goes first. She says "Cheese."

Doris goes second. She says "Cheese."

Freddy goes next. He says "Parmesan."

I guess that's *cheese* in Italian.

Eric goes next. He doesn't say anything, but he doesn't put a hat in front of his face ... Chicken!

Derek and Randy go and then the photographer says, "Next."

I step into the limelight. Boy, it's bright. I can't see a thing. I'm about to take a heroic pose when the photographer says, "Next."

CLICK!

That's it? It's over? I don't even know when he took the picture. I don't even know *if* he took a picture.

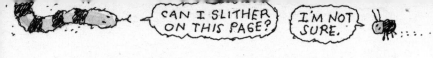

Oh, well. It's history now. My one moment of fame went by so fast—I think I missed it.

Next, we line up to take our class picture. We all go for it!

CHAPTER 17
HOLD THAT POSE!

Two weeks later, we get the pictures. Here is our class photo. I thought you'd like to see it.

WHAT A GOOD-LOOKING GROUP.

Here's my picture, too.

Oh, well. There's always next year.

Put your school photo here.